W9-CCR-456

STAR WARS®

THE CLONE WARS™

R2-D2's Adventure

Adapted by Kirsten Mayer

Grosset & Dunlap • LucasBooks

GROSSET & DUNLAP
Published by the Penguin Group
Penguin Group (USA) Inc., 375 Hudson Street, New York, New York 10014, USA
Penguin Group (Canada), 90 Eglinton Avenue East, Suite 700,
Toronto, Ontario M4P 2Y3, Canada
(a division of Pearson Penguin Canada Inc.)
Penguin Books Ltd., 80 Strand, London WC2R 0RL, England
Penguin Group Ireland, 25 St. Stephen's Green, Dublin 2, Ireland
(a division of Penguin Books Ltd.)
Penguin Group (Australia), 250 Camberwell Road, Camberwell,
Victoria 3124, Australia
(a division of Pearson Australia Group Pty. Ltd.)
Penguin Books India Pvt. Ltd., 11 Community Centre, Panchsheel Park,
New Delhi—110 017, India
Penguin Group (NZ), 67 Apollo Drive, Rosedale, North Shore 0632, New Zealand
(a division of Pearson New Zealand Ltd.)
Penguin Books (South Africa) (Pty.) Ltd., 24 Sturdee Avenue,
Rosebank, Johannesburg 2196, South Africa

Penguin Books Ltd., Registered Offices:
80 Strand, London WC2R 0RL, England

This book is published in partnership with LucasBooks, a division of Lucasfilm Ltd.

ISBN: 978-0-448-45222-7   10 9 8 7 6 5 4 3 2 1

3 1984 00287 6363

WHO'S WHO

Ahsoka Tano: Anakin's Padawan. She is training to become a Jedi Knight.

Anakin Skywalker: Jedi Knight and a general in the Republic Army.

Clone Captain Rex: Captain in the clone army of the Republic.

General Grievous: A cybernetic monster and an enemy of the Jedi and the Republic.

Gha Nachkt: A Trandoshan scavenger. His loyalty is easily bought.

Obi-Wan Kenobi: A Jedi Master and Anakin's former teacher.

R2-D2: Anakin's trusty astromech droid.

R3-S6: A new astromech droid with a secret. Ahsoka nicknames him Goldie.

General Grievous and his droid army had won a
series of battles against the Republic. Near the
planet Bothawui, Grievous launched his latest atta[c]
Anakin Skywalker, Padawan Ahsoka Tano, and the
clone army stood their ground against Grievous.

As his ship exploded around him, General Grievous escaped in a starfighter.

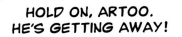

HOLD ON, ARTOO.
HE'S GETTING AWAY!

BEEP!
BEEP!

Anakin Skywalker and
R2-D2 chased Grievous
as he powered up his
hyperdrive.

MORE SPEED, ARTOO!

BEEP! BOO

A Separatist ship exploded around them!

KA-BOOM!

A chunk of the other ship hit the wing of Skywalker's starfighter!

KA-CHINK!

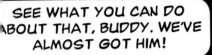
SEE WHAT YOU CAN DO ABOUT THAT, BUDDY. WE'VE ALMOST GOT HIM!

ZOOOM!

But R2-D2 couldn't fix it—the damage was too bad!

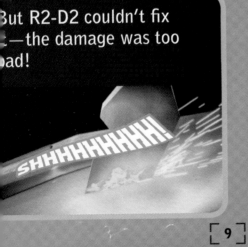
SHHHHHHHH!

BEEEEEP!

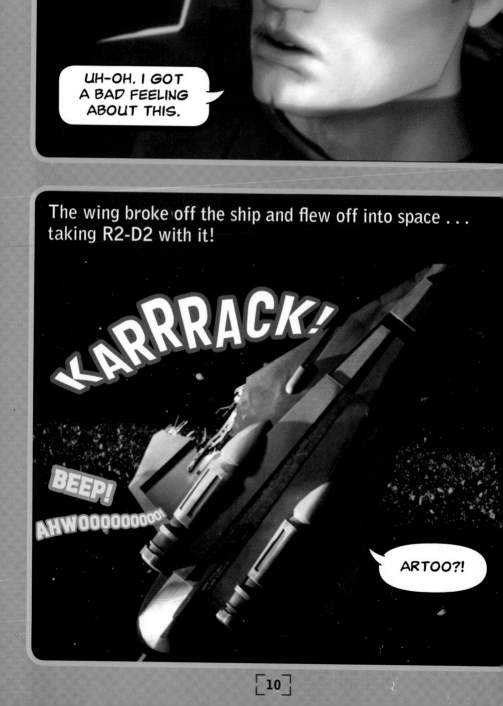

The wing broke off the ship and flew off into space . . .
taking R2-D2 with it!

the war room, Obi-Wan checked in by hologram.

CONGRATULATIONS ON YOUR VICTORY, ANAKIN.

THANK YOU, BUT I LOST ARTOO IN THE FIELD.

WELL, R2 UNITS ARE A DIME A DOZEN. I'M SURE YOU'LL FIND A REPLACEMENT.

IT'S JUST THAT . . . UM . . . I DIDN'T WIPE ARTOO'S MEMORY.

GASP!

WHAT?! HE'S STILL PROGRAMMED WITH ALL OUR TACTICS AND BASE LOCATIONS?!

FIND THAT DROID. NECKS MIGHT VE WELL DEPEND O

RIGHT AWAY!

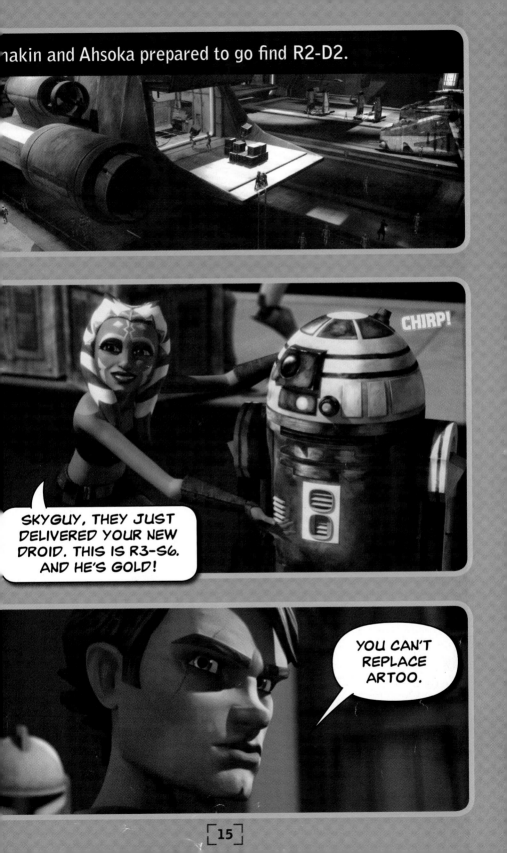

Among the space debris, they found the wing from Anakin's ship . . .

. . . but no R2-D2

HE'S GOT TO BE AROUND HERE SOMEWHERE.

THE SCANNERS AR PICKING UP A SHIP

AN R SERIES? NO. WE'VE GOT SOME FINE T-SEVENS.

POOKUMS HERE REALLY WANTS AN R2. SHE LOST THE LAST ONE. NOW . . .

POOKUMS?!

. . . LET'S SEE HOW MUCH I HAVE HERE TO PAY YOU.

CLINK!

TELL YOU WHAT, I MAY HAVE AN R2 UNIT BURIED SOMEWHERE IN THE HOLD. FOLLOW ME.

HEH HEH HEHE!

ha Nachkt took them
o the hold of his ship to
earch for R2-D2 . . .

. . . but all they found
were assassin droids!

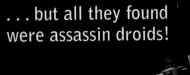

WHIRRRRR!

FVOOM!

FWOOSH!

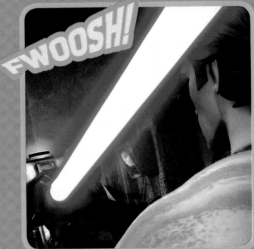

LET'S GET
OUT OF HERE.

Skywalker and
his Padawan
left without
finding their
friend.

I TOLD YOU
ERE WERE NO
DROIDS DOWN
ERE! LOOK AT
IS MESS YOU
MADE!

What the Jedi didn't realize was that Gha Nachkt *did* have R2-D2 onboard . . .

. . . but he already had a buyer.

I'VE GOT THE MERCHANDISE YOU WERE LOOKING FOR. IT MUST BE VALUABLE— A JEDI CAME LOOKING FOR IT.

YOU BRING THAT R2 UNIT TO ME, YOU SLIME! OR ELSE!

As the scavenger ship zoomed to meet General Grievous, R2-D2 tried to send a distress call.

BEEP!
BOOP!

WHIRRRR!

Gha Nachkt landed at the secret Separatist base, Skytop Station.

THIS IS THE DROID YOU WANTED, GENERAL.

WHAT SECRETS DO YOU CARRY, MY LITTLE FRIEND?

BOOP!

R2-D2 was in serious trouble! Meanwhile, thanks to the little droid's distress call, the Jedi discovered the secret base.

Skywalker and his team snuck onto the base to destroy it.

AHSOKA, TAKE THE SQUAD AND BLOW UP THE REACTORS. WE'LL MEET IN THE LANDING BAY.

I HOPE YOU FIND ARTOO IN ONE PIECE.

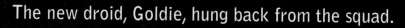

BEEP!

BEEP!

REPORT, AGENT ARTHREE.

THE JEDI ARE HERE
DELAY THEM UNTIL
GET THERE.

GOLDIE, WHAT ARE
YOU DOING BACK
THERE? COME ON!

SOUND THE ALARM AND TAKE THIS R2 UNIT TO MY SHIP!

The guards picked up R2-D2 and carried him to General Grievous's ship.

BOOP!

WAA-OOO

Anakin found his friend!

ARTOO!

THANKS, ARTOO.

BEEP!
BEEP!

IT'S GREAT TO SEE YOU, TOO, BUDDY.

LET'S GO FIND EVERYONE ELSE AND GET OUT OF HERE.

The mission was a success and everyone escaped to the *Twilight*.

I CAN'T BELIEVE THAT GOLD DROID WAS A SPY!

BEEP!

I GUESS GOLDIE FOOLED ALL OF US.

ANAKIN, YOU RISKED THE MISSION, YOUR MEN, EVEN YOUR PADAWAN, ALL TO SAVE A *DROID*!

I KNEW AHSOKA WOULD COMPLETE THE MISSION. AND ARTOO IS MORE THAN A DROID. HE'S A FRIEND.

CHIRP!